Sky Scare

by Bobbi JG Weiss & David Cody Weiss

Illustrated by Artful Doodlers

SCHOLASTIC INC.

New York   Toronto   London   Auckland   Sydney
Mexico City   New Delhi   Hong Kong   Buenos Aires

Published by Scholastic Inc.,
90 Old Sherman Turnpike, Danbury, Connecticut 06816.

SCHOLASTIC and associated logos are trademarks
and/or registered trademarks of Scholastic Inc.

ISBN 0-439-56272-4

First Scholastic Printing, November 2003

Chapters

10

Sam Dullard woke up with a start.

"Whoa," he thought. "What a nightmare!"

"Good morning, sleepy dude!" Otto Rocket called to Sam. "Is everybody ready to fly high today?"

"Let's do it, Rocket Boy!" said Otto's sister, Reggie.

"And I'm going to capture it all on my Twister-Vision Skycam!" promised their friend Twister Rodriguez.

"Hurry up and get dressed, Squidman," Twister told Sam. "Raymundo is waiting."

Raymundo was Ray Rocket, Reggie's and Otto's dad. Ray and his friend Tito Makani had driven the kids to Vista Cliffs to camp and go hang gliding. Talk about an extreme adventure!

Sam had only one problem . . .

Sam was afraid of heights. "Everyone already thinks I'm the Face-Plant King," he thought. "Why am I so afraid? I want to be brave like they are!"

But Sam didn't feel very brave. "What am I going to do?" he wondered.

Ray and his friend Hawk were waiting in the clearing. Hawk was president of the Skyhawk Club and knew all there was to know about hang gliding.

"We're going tandem flying," Hawk explained. "That means you'll ride in a glider designed to carry two people—you and a Skyhawk pilot."

"You'll wear helmets, goggles, and a parachute in case of emergency," Hawk continued. "We've got boo-wah conditions today, which means flying will be good."

Hawk smiled. "So let's go! Nobody wants to be a launch potato."

Otto and Reggie each ran toward a glider.

"What's the wait, boys?" Hawk asked Twister and Sam, who hadn't moved.

"I want to get some juicy shots of Otto and Reggie taking off first," explained Twister.

Hawk turned to Sam. "You're my flight partner, Sam. Do you want to strap in now?"

"Uh . . . I want to watch the launches, too," Sam said.

"Raymundo is flying solo," said Twister. "What about you, Tito?"

"Oh, I don't fly anymore, little cuz," Tito replied. "As the ancient Hawaiians said: 'The seagull soars where the whale cannot.'"

"I'm going to go set up my first shot," Twister said. "Man, can you believe we have to leap over a cliff to launch? What a rush!"

Sam gulped. "Yeah. I'm, uh, really stoked."

"Look out, fly dudes, here I go!" shouted
Otto as he and his pilot ran toward the cliff.

"Go, Otto, go! Go, Otto, go!" everyone
cheered.

Twister filmed the launch with his
video camera.

"And we're off!" Otto shouted from the sky with glee.

Then it was Reggie's turn. "Woo-hoo!" she laughed. "See you groundhogs later!"

Sam moaned to himself. "Ohhh, I can't do this . . . "

Twister scrambled up a tree with his camera.

"Hey, little cuz," Tito called up to Twister. "What are you doing?"

"I want to video Raymundo's jump from up here," replied Twister. "It'll make an awesome shot!"

Next it was Ray's turn. "Cowabunga!" he whooped as he leaped off the cliff.

"Race an eagle for me, bro!" Tito called to his friend.

"What a shot!" Twister said happily.

"This is going to be my best—"

"Uh-oh!" Twister lost his balance. "Help!" he cried, tumbling out of the tree.

Chapter 4
Totally Twisted Twister

"Man, this is bogus!" Twister complained as Hawk bandaged his ankle. "Can I still go hang gliding?"

"Sorry, buddy," Hawk replied. "It wouldn't be safe."

"I'm sorry, Twist," said Sam, as he wished deep inside that he was the one with the twisted ankle.

"Here you go, Squidman," said Twister, handing his camera to Sam. "I'm counting on you."

"*Me?*" Sam squealed. "You want *me* to film stuff? From up in the air?"

"Don't worry, Sam," said Hawk. "You'll get some good shots. Maybe we'll even catch a thermal and speck out." He smiled at Sam's confused look. "That means we'd go so high we'd look like a little speck to anybody down here. You'd get some great video."

Sam thought to himself, "Yeah—or hurl."

Finally, the big moment came. "I can do this," Sam told himself. "I can do this."

But just before they reached the cliff—

Sam yelled, "STOP! I can't do this!"

"Mr. Hawk," Sam began to explain, "I . . . I'm afraid of heights."

"Why didn't you tell anyone?" asked Hawk.

"I wanted to but . . . well, I was trying to be brave." When Hawk didn't laugh at him, Sam added, "And I didn't want to let Twister down."

Sam sighed. "Now I've let us both down."

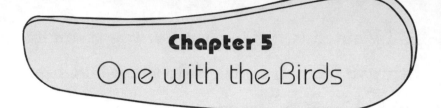

Chapter 5
One with the Birds

Later, Tito found Sam sitting by himself.
"Hawk told me why you didn't fly," Tito
began. "Don't feel bad, little cuz. Here."

"A feather?" asked Sam.

"This isn't just any feather,"
Tito explained. "Remember, I used to

hang glide, too," Tito said. "When I carried this good-luck feather, it gave lightness to my being and bravery to my heart. With it, I could fly like an eagle."

"Flying isn't just something you do, little cuz," Tito went on. "It's something you feel. When you're high in the air, your spirit is free to soar."

"Wow, that's really cool," said Sam, taking the feather in his hand. "Okay, I'll give it another try!"

Hawk and Sam once again strapped into the glider.

Sam closed his eyes. "I can do it, I can do it!" he thought, as he held tightly to Tito's good-luck feather.

"Go, Sam, go! Go, Sam, go!" cheered Tito and the Skyhawks, as the pair ran to the edge of the cliff and leaped off.

Suddenly everything became quiet.

Sam opened his eyes and gasped. "Whoa, it's beautiful up here!" he exclaimed.

Just then the glider dipped with the wind, and the feather fell out of Sam's hand.

"Oh no!" cried Sam, as all his fear came rushing back. "Mr. Hawk, we have to go back! Please, stop! Heeeeeelp!"

"Easy there, Sam," Hawk said, his voice sure and steady. "Flying is new to you, that's all. If you're scared, all you have to do is howl."

"Howl?" Sam asked.

"When you howl, you give your fear to the wind," Hawk explained. "I'll start, and you join in. Aaoooo!" howled Hawk.

Sam felt silly, but he was willing to try.

"Aaoooo!" he howled.

The valley echoed their cries. Sam heard it and began to laugh.

"My fear is in the wind, and my spirit is soaring," Sam thought. "Man, flying is GREAT!"

Afterward, Tito congratulated Sam. "But I lost your good-luck feather," Sam confessed.

"Don't worry," said Tito, a smile spreading across his face. "It was just a feather I found on the ground this morning."

"You mean it *didn't* have special powers?" Sam asked, surprised.

Tito shrugged. "Who's to say? It worked, didn't it?"

The next day, back in Ocean Shores, Sam showed the video to his friends.

"Whoa," said Twister. "Did that eagle fly right next to you, Squidman?"

"Yup," replied Sam proudly.

"Hey, Rocket Girl," Otto said to his sister. "This shot qualifies you for the Dork Face of the Year Award!"

"Oh, yeah?" said Reggie. "You look ready to toss some major cookies in this shot, Otto-man!"

"Well, I'm going to outfly all you guys when we go hang gliding again next month," Twister bragged.

"Just stay out of the trees 'til then, okay?" Tito told him.

Just then a strange sound started coming
from the TV.

"Say, what's that noise?" asked Ray.

Sam knew what it was. The video
microphone had picked up his howling with
Hawk. But Sam didn't tell anybody.

"Well, whatever it is," Ray said, "you did a good job with the video, Sam."

"Only good?" said Sam. "I think I did a *howling* good job!"